OLYMPIC SPORTS

OLYMPIC TRACK AND FIELD

BY LUKE HANLON

SportsZone
An Imprint of Abdo Publishing
abdobooks.com

abdobooks.com

Published by Abdo Publishing, a division of ABDO, PO Box 398166, Minneapolis, Minnesota 55439.

Printed in the United States of America, North Mankato, Minnesota.
102024
012025

Cover Photo: Cameron Spencer/Getty Images Sport/Getty Images
Interior Photos: Olivier Morin/AFP/Getty Images, 5; Mark Dadswell/Getty Images Sport/Getty Images, 6; Ian MacNicol/Getty Images Sport/Getty Images, 8; Emmanuel Dunand/AFP/Getty Images, 10; Print Collector/Heritage Images/Hulton Archive/Getty Images, 13; ullstein bild Dtl./Getty Images, 15, 25; RDB/ullstein bild Dtl./Getty Images, 16; Tony Duffy/Allsport/Getty Images Sports/Getty Images, 18; Wang Lili/Xinhua News Agency/Getty Images, 20; Bernat Armangue/AP Images, 21; Bettmann/Getty Images, 23, 26; Smith Archive/Alamy, 29; Tony Duffy/Allsport/Hulton Archive/Getty Images, 31; David Madison/Getty Images Sport/Getty Images, 32, 35; Ed Reinke/AP Images, 37; Patrick Smith/Getty Images Sport/Getty Images, 39; Charly Triballeau/AFP/Getty Images, 41; Michael Steele/Getty Images Sport/Getty Images, 42; Cameron Spencer/Getty Images Sport/Getty Images, 45

Editor: Haley Williams
Series Designer: Karli Kruse

Library of Congress Control Number: 2024939389

Publisher's Cataloging-in-Publication Data

Names: Hanlon, Luke, author.
Title: Olympic track and field / by Luke Hanlon
Description: Minneapolis, Minnesota: ABDO Publishing, 2025 | Series: Olympic sports | Includes online resources and index.
Identifiers: ISBN 9781098295523 (lib. bdg.) | ISBN 9798384916529 (ebook)
Subjects: LCSH: Olympic games--Juvenile literature. | Track and field--Juvenile literature. | Athletics (Track athletics)--Juvenile literature. | Olympians (Olympic athletes) --Juvenile literature. | Olympics--History--Juvenile literature. | Sports--Juvenile literature.
Classification: DDC 796.42--dc23

TABLE OF CONTENTS

CHAPTER 1 LIGHTNING BOLT

Usain Bolt placed both of his hands down on the track. The Jamaican sprinter was seconds away from competing in his first Olympic final at the 2008 Games in Beijing, China. Three months earlier, he had set the world record in the 100-meter dash. Now track-and-field fans wanted to see the 21-year-old Bolt on the Olympic stage.

The starting pistol blasted. As he often did, the long and lean Bolt started slowly out of the blocks. At the 50-meter mark, multiple runners were running alongside Bolt. They didn't stay with him for long, though. At 6 feet, 5 inches tall, Bolt used his long strides to break away from the pack. With 20 meters to go, Bolt knew he had won the race. He couldn't contain his excitement. Bolt extended his arms out wide. Then he beat his chest in celebration as he crossed the finish line.

Bolt easily won gold. His time of 9.69 seconds also broke his own world record. He could have run an even faster time

Jamaica's Usain Bolt wore gold track spikes in all of his finals at the 2008 Olympics.

Bolt set his first world record in the 100-meter sprint in May 2008 in New York. A few months later at the Olympics, he became the first person to run the 100 in under 9.70 seconds.

if he had not slowed down to celebrate. But Bolt did not care. He said he wasn't focused on breaking records. All he wanted to do was win gold. The sprinter, fittingly known as "Lightning Bolt," had captured Jamaica's first Olympic gold in the men's 100-meter. And Bolt didn't slow down anytime soon.

MAKE IT A DOUBLE

Although Bolt's record-breaking performance was thrilling, he did not consider the 100-meter to be his best event. He had only started training for the 100-meter sprint a year before the 2008 Olympics. In fact, his coach didn't want him to run it. But Bolt thought the fast-paced race suited him.

Before picking up the 100, Bolt solely focused on the 200-meter dash. Opponents struggled to keep up with Bolt.

He appeared to glide around the track. Almost everyone expected him to win gold in the 200 at the 2008 Games. In Olympic sprinting events, runners must advance past two heats to make it to the final. In Bolt's first two 200 heats, he jogged through the finish line to save his energy.

The final for the 200 came four days after his victory in the 100. Bolt always raced with confidence. That was on full display before the 200-meter final even began. At the starting blocks, Bolt fixed his hair and pointed toward the big screen in the stadium. He wanted to put on a show for the fans in the stands and the millions of people watching from home.

Bolt did just that. This time, he burst out of the starting blocks. When he reached the final 100 meters, Bolt already had a comfortable lead. He surged down the homestretch with no other runner close to him. Instead of slowing down, Bolt stormed past the finish line. He then put his hands into the air to celebrate another gold-medal performance. His time of 19.30 seconds had set another world record. He became the first sprinter to win gold medals in the 100-meter and 200-meter races at the same Olympics since 1984.

When Bolt received his gold medal, he stretched out his arms to look like a lightning bolt. The crowd erupted in cheers. People around the world had witnessed the beginning of a legendary career.

Bolt's signature victory pose, called "To Di World" or "Lightning Bolt," originated from a popular Jamaican dance move.

THE GREATEST OF ALL TIME

Heading into the 2012 Olympics in London, England, Bolt had become a global superstar. After his success at the 2008 Games, Bolt reached a new level at the 2009 World Championships. He shattered his 100-meter world record with a new time of 9.58 seconds. Then he sprinted the 200-meter in 19.19, also a world record.

The 2012 Games became a chance for Bolt to cement his star status. Almost everyone expected him to defend his golds in the 100 and 200. However, he faced tough competition in the 100-meter final. Fellow Jamaican Yohan Blake came into the Olympics as the defending world champion in the 100. Bolt himself said Blake could beat him. Meanwhile, former world and Olympic champion Justin Gatlin of the United States had returned from a doping ban hoping to win gold.

Despite facing motivated challengers, Bolt couldn't be caught. He burst ahead of the pack in the final stretch of the race. Bolt lunged through the finish line to break his own Olympic record with a time of 9.63 seconds. Blake settled for silver while Gatlin took home the bronze.

In the 200-meter final, Blake came close to spoiling Bolt's attempt to repeat. Despite Bolt dealing with a back injury, he broke away in the homestretch of the race to finish first. He became the first person to win gold in both the 100 and 200 in two straight Olympics.

Bolt still had one more race in London. Typically, track meets end with the 4x400-meter relay race, including in the Olympics. Not at the 2012 Games, though. Instead, the men's 4x100-meter relay was the final race. Track fans wanted to end on a high note and see Bolt run one more time. He did not disappoint them. When Blake handed the baton to Bolt to close the race, Jamaica and the United States were neck and neck. Then Bolt left American anchor Ryan Bailey in the dust. Bolt won his third gold of the 2012 Games. He also helped Jamaica set a world-record time of 36.84 seconds.

After the 2012 Olympics, there was little doubt that Bolt was one of the greatest sprinters of all time. He entered the 2016 Games in Rio de Janeiro, Brazil, with nothing left to prove. The only thing Bolt could do was add to his medal collection. American Carl Lewis had won six sprinting medals during his Olympic career from 1984 to 1996. No male sprinter had won more. Bolt had a chance to surpass that in Rio.

Bolt, then 29 years old, started his final Olympics with the 100. Gatlin returned as a threat to Bolt's title. The American led

Along with his Olympic success, Bolt, *right*, won 11 world titles during his career.

for most of the race. Then, Bolt surged in the final 20 meters to win gold again. Bolt was now the first sprinter to ever win three straight Olympic golds in the 100. Four days later, Bolt led the pack during the entire 200 final. No man had ever won two Olympic gold medals in a row in that race. Bolt defended his title to win his third straight gold medal.

Bolt ran his final Olympic race two days later. However, helping Jamaica defend its gold in the 4x100 proved to be no easy task for him and his teammates. The United States had beaten the Jamaicans in the same event at a major international event in 2015. When Bolt received the baton, the anchors for Japan and the United States were right with him. But as he had done throughout his career, Bolt burst ahead of his competition. The win secured Bolt's eighth gold medal. And it further cemented his status as an Olympic legend.

UNOFFICIAL THREE-PEAT

After winning two individual golds at the 2008 Olympics, Usain Bolt ran the third leg for Jamaica in the 4x100-meter relay. The race was close when Bolt received the baton. Once he handed it off to teammate Asafa Powell, Jamaica had a big lead. Powell finished the race to give Jamaica a world record of 37.1 seconds. However, the team's gold medal was stripped in 2017 due to one Jamaican runner failing a drug test.

CHAPTER 2

GREEK ORIGINS

The history of track and field traces back thousands of years to ancient Greece. In 776 BCE, people from across Greece traveled to the city of Olympia to compete in a race. That event became known as the first Olympic Games. Olympia began hosting the Games every four years. This tradition lasted for centuries. Field events were added over time as the Games grew more and more popular. These events included the broad jump, discus, and javelin.

The ancient Olympic Games ended around 393 CE. Modern track and field did not become the sport it is today until the 1800s. It started gaining widespread popularity during that time. In 1864, England's Cambridge University and Oxford University competed in the first collegiate track-and-field meet. Two years later, England hosted its first amateur national championships for the sport.

Discobolus by Myron is an ancient Greek statue of a discus thrower. The original statue was sculpted around 450 BCE.

Track and field's new popularity spread from England to the United States in the late 1800s. The United States began hosting collegiate track meets in 1873. Around that same time, a French educator named Pierre de Coubertin wanted to create an event that connected the world through sports. So, he came up with the modern Olympic Games, which were based off the ancient Olympics. The first modern Games were held in Athens, Greece, in 1896. Track and field was one of the sports featured. All the track-and-field events from the 1896 Games are still competed in the Olympics today.

LOCAL HERO

In 490 BCE, a messenger named Pheidippides ran 25 miles (40.2 km) from the Greek city of Marathon to Athens. He told people that the Greeks had beat the Persians in a battle. He then died of exhaustion. When Athens hosted the first modern Olympics in 1896, Pheidippides was honored with a race that was the same distance he ran. It was called the marathon. Greece's Spyridon Louis won the race by more than seven minutes. At the 1908 Olympics in London, officials changed the distance of the marathon to 26.2 miles (42.2 km).

WOMEN JOIN THE RACE

Women were not allowed to compete at the first modern Olympics in 1896. Many people at the time thought sports were too tiring for women to participate in. The Amateur Athletic Union became the governing body of track and field in the United States in 1887. In 1922, the organization allowed women to start competing in track and field. However, women did not begin to participate in Olympic track and field until 1928.

The 1928 Games in Amsterdam, Netherlands, featured 100-meter and 800-meter races for women, as well as the 4x100 relay, high jump, and discus events. American Betty Robinson won gold in the 100. That made the 16-year-old the first woman to claim an Olympic gold medal in track and field. Germany's Lina Radke set a world record in the 800.

In addition to her gold in the 100, the United States' Betty Robinson, *second from left*, also won a silver medal in the women's 4x100 relay at the 1928 Olympics.

The hammer throw is a field event in which athletes throw a metal ball attached to a long wire and a hand grip.

However, the press did not focus on Radke's accomplishment. One reporter incorrectly wrote that multiple women did not finish the race. Others exaggerated how tired the women were afterwards. As a result, the women's 800 didn't appear in the Olympics again until the 1960 Games in Rome, Italy.

RUN, JUMP, AND THROW

Track and field at the Olympics has not changed much since the 1928 Games. Races ranged from 100 meters all the way to a marathon, which is 26.2 miles (42.2 km). Those remain the shortest and longest running races held at the Olympics today. Not all races are just running around the track, though. Athletes must jump over 10 hurdles in hurdling events. In relay races, competitors run with a baton that they hand off to a teammate to continue the race. Athletes can also participate in the steeplechase and race walk events at the Games.

In the field at the 1928 Olympics, men took part in the throwing events of discus, hammer, javelin, and shot put. Those Games also featured the high jump, long jump, triple jump, and pole vault. Over time, each of these events were also offered for women. The 2024 Olympics in Paris, France, featured 48 track-and-field events, with 24 for men and 24 for women. That marked the first time there were an equal number of events for men and women at the Olympics.

West Germany's Jürgen Hingsen competes in the pole vault during the men's decathlon at the 1984 Olympics in Los Angeles.

Multisport events have always carried particular significance in the Olympics. During the ancient Games, the Greeks held a competition called the pentathlon. It consisted of five events. Athletes competed in a sprint race, the long jump, discus, javelin, and a wrestling match.

The first modern Olympics did not feature the pentathlon. However, the 1912 Games in Stockholm, Sweden, introduced the world to a new multisport event. This was the men's decathlon, which consists of 10 events across two days. On the first day, athletes compete in the 100-meter race, long jump, shot put, high jump, and 400-meter race. Then they participate in the 110-meter hurdles, discus, pole vault, javelin, and 1,500-meter race on the second day. Athletes earn points for each event. The competitor with the most points after all 10 events takes the gold. To win an Olympic decathlon, athletes need speed, strength, jumping ability, and endurance.

A women's pentathlon was added to the Olympic program at the 1964 Games in Tokyo, Japan. That year, athletes competed in the 80-meter hurdles, shot put, long jump, high jump, and the 200-meter race. In 1984, the heptathlon replaced the pentathlon in the Olympics. In the heptathlon, the hurdles race was extended to 100 meters. The javelin and 800-meter sprint were added as events as well. As in the decathlon, the athlete with the most points from the seven events wins gold. Today, men compete in the decathlon at the Games, while women compete in the heptathlon.

TOP OF THE SPORT

The United States has been the most successful country in the history of Olympic track and field. In fact, no other country has come close to matching the Americans' success. In 2024, the United States won its 862nd Olympic track-and-field medal. The next closest country is Great Britain with more than 220 total medals.

The United States does not dominate every event at the Games, though. The African countries Ethiopia and Kenya haven't had a lot of success in many Olympic sports over the years. But they both have a rich history in distance running. In the 3,000-meter steeplechase, Kenya has won 11 golds and 29 total medals. In races 5,000 meters or longer, Ethiopia has claimed 24 golds and 56 total medals.

Finland has a population of about 5.6 million people. More than 20 US states have a larger population than the European country. Yet Finland has been a force in men's javelin. Finnish men have won 22 Olympic medals in the event. And the

The 4x400 mixed relay race was added to the Olympic program for the Tokyo, Japan, Games in 2021. Two men and two women from each country compete in this event.

Haruka Kitaguchi secured Japan's first gold medal in the javelin at the 2024 Olympics.

country's seven gold medals in men's javelin were won by six different athletes. Meanwhile, the Germans have thrived in the women's javelin. Women from Germany have won five Olympic golds and 16 total medals in the event.

CHAPTER 3

EARLY STARS

The odds of American Ray Ewry becoming an Olympian were extremely low. When Ewry was a kid, he contracted polio. The disease left him in a wheelchair. Some doctors thought he would never walk again. However, Ewry eventually did more than just walk. He became an elite jumper. He showed off his leaping ability at the 1900 Olympics in Paris.

Ewry competed in the standing high jump, standing long jump, and standing triple jump. He won gold in all three events. Then he defended those titles four years later in St. Louis. The standing triple jump didn't appear in the 1908 Olympics in London. So, Ewry had to settle for two gold medals at those Games. After the 1912 Olympics, all jumping events changed to incorporate running starts.

A new star emerged at the 1920 Olympics in Antwerp, Belgium. Finnish distance runner Paavo Nurmi won three golds and a silver in his Olympic debut. Four years later in Paris, he

Ray Ewry of the United States ended his career with eight gold medals across three Olympic Games.

ALL-AROUND ATHLETE

American Jim Thorpe showcased his elite athletic skills at the 1912 Olympics in Stockholm. Thorpe finished first in four of the five pentathlon events to win gold. He then crushed his competition in the decathlon. Thorpe won gold while beating the silver medalist by almost 700 points. And he set a decathlon world record. That record stood until American Bob Mathias broke it at the 1952 Games in Helsinki, Finland.

defied what many thought the human body was capable of. In the span of four days, Nurmi ran five races and more than 20,000 meters (65,600 ft). He won gold in all five races. That didn't satisfy Nurmi, though. He also wanted to defend his gold in the 10,000-meter race. But Finnish officials feared that would be too much running in a short span. So, they didn't enter him in the race. Instead, Nurmi ran a 10,000-meter race back home in Finland after the 1924 Games. And he finished it with a new world record.

Fellow Finnish distance runner Ville Ritola won gold in the 10,000-meter race at the 1924 Games. He also finished second to Nurmi in the 5,000-meter and the cross-country race. Then, the duo won gold together in the cross-country team race. Four years later, the "Flying Finns" battled in Amsterdam. They competed against each other in the 5,000 and 10,000. Nurmi reclaimed his 10,000-meter title, with Ritola taking the silver. The reverse result happened in the 5,000. Ritola finished his

Olympic career with five golds and eight total medals. Nurmi ended with nine golds and a record 12 track-and-field medals.

GROUNDBREAKING PERFORMANCES

When Berlin, Germany, hosted the 1936 Olympics, dictator Adolf Hitler ran the country. Some countries considered boycotting the Games because of Hitler's racist and politically dangerous views. The United States was one of those countries. However, the Americans did end up competing in those Games.

That set the stage for American Jesse Owens. A Black athlete, Owens defied Hitler's racist beliefs. With Hitler watching from the stands, Owens dominated every event he competed in. He won gold in the 100, 200, and long jump in a

American Jesse Owens, *right*, set an Olympic record in the 100-meter dash and a world record in the 200-meter dash at the 1936 Games.

Wilma Rudolph, *middle*, of the United States shakes hands with Great Britain's Dorothy Hyman, *left*, and Italy's Giuseppina Leone during the women's 100-meter medal ceremony at the 1960 Olympics.

three-day span. Then Owens ran the first leg of the 4x100 relay. The United States won gold with ease, beating silver medalist Italy by more than a second. Owens helped the US team set a world record of 39.8 seconds.

Wilma Rudolph grew up idolizing Owens. However, it seemed impossible that she could ever become an Olympic sprinter herself. Rudolph was diagnosed with polio at a young age. There was a chance she would never walk again. Her parents and 21 siblings took care of her. By the time she was 11, Rudolph was playing basketball. She became an All-American in high school. Team USA track-and-field coach Ed Temple thought Rudolph would make a great athlete in that sport, too. So, he recruited her. After high school, Rudolph competed in track and field at Tennessee State University, where Temple served as the head coach of the track team.

Rudolph ended up competing against college athletes while she was in high school. She made her Olympic debut at 16 in the 1956 Games in Melbourne, Australia. She helped the US women win bronze in the 4x100 relay. Rudolph then became one of the brightest stars at the Rome Olympics four years later. She won gold in the 100, 200, and 4x100. That made her the first American woman to win three golds in one Olympics. She also set multiple world records in the process. After the Games, Rudolph dedicated her performance to Jesse Owens.

Four years after coaching Rudolph at the 1960 Olympics, Temple got to coach another iconic sprinter. Like Rudolph, Wyomia Tyus attended Tennessee State. She then followed in Rudolph's footsteps at the 1964 Olympics in Tokyo. Before the 100 final, Temple told Tyus she had a chance to medal. Tyus corrected him and said she had a chance to win. She ended up being right, as she won gold in the event.

UPSET FOR THE AGES

Not many people had heard of Billy Mills before the 1964 Olympics. The American entered the men's 10,000-meter final with a personal-best time almost a minute slower than the other runners in the event. However, Mills stayed near the front of the pack for most of the race. Then a late burst made him the first American to win gold in the 10,000.

At the 1968 Olympics in Mexico City, Mexico, Tyus had a chance to make history. Nobody had ever repeated as the Olympic champion in the 100. Before the final, Tyus danced at the start line to calm her nerves. That worked wonders for her. Tyus defended her gold medal with a world record of 11.08 seconds.

BREAKING RECORDS

While Tyus made history on the track in 1968, many of the famous performances from those Games came in field events. Mexico City is about 7,350 feet (2,240 m) above sea level. The high elevation led to some massive jumps. None were more impressive than American Bob Beamon's long jump. On his first attempt in the men's long jump, Beamon leaped so far that his jump couldn't be measured right away. After a long delay, he found out he had jumped 8.90 meters (29.2 ft). That shattered the men's long jump record by 0.55 meters (1.8 ft). Beamon couldn't believe it. He was so shocked that he collapsed to the ground. No one came close to his winning jump.

Multiple world records fell in the men's triple jump during the 1968 Games. The bronze and silver medalist each broke the previous world record. But neither could match Viktor Saneyev of the Soviet Union. He set a world record with his third jump.

The Soviet Union's Viktor Saneyev set three world records in the triple jump during his career. His last world record was set in 1972, when he jumped 17.44 meters (57.22 ft).

Then he broke it again on his sixth and final jump. His leap of 17.39 meters (57 ft) secured the gold in a historic event. Saneyev went on to win gold in the triple jump in the next two Olympics as well.

While Saneyev was starting a golden streak, another one was extended in Mexico City. American Al Oerter won gold in the men's discus at the 1956 Olympics. And he set an Olympic record while winning it. Oerter achieved both feats again in 1960 and 1964. Then, in 1968, he unleashed a throw of 64.78 meters (212.5 ft). That shattered his own Olympic record by 3.78 meters (12.4 ft). The win made Oerter the first track-and-field athlete to secure four straight Olympic titles.

WOMEN'S REVOLUTION

Even though women first competed in Olympic track and field in 1928, they had significantly fewer events to participate in than men. The Olympics slowly began adding more running events for women throughout the years. By the 1984 Games in Los Angeles, there were 12 races for women. The marathon was one significant new event for women that year.

Leading up to the 1984 Olympics, American Joan Benoit was the favorite to win gold in the marathon. A year earlier, she had broken the women's marathon world record by eight minutes. However, she suffered a knee injury just one month before the

Joan Benoit was inducted into the US Olympic and Paralympic Hall of Fame in 2008.

US Olympic Trials. She had surgery 17 days before the Trials. People had doubts whether Benoit could even run, let alone qualify for the Games. She put those doubts to rest by winning the Trials. Then she crossed the finish line during the Games more than a minute ahead of the silver medalist. A crowd of 77,000 fans roared for Benoit as she became the first woman to win Olympic gold in the women's marathon.

Another change to the Olympic program for women in 1984 was the heptathlon replacing the pentathlon. Jackie Joyner-Kersee fell five points short of winning the gold in the heptathlon that year. When the American competed again at the 1988 Games in Seoul, South Korea, taking home gold

American Jackie Joyner-Kersee finished her Olympic career with six medals, including three golds.

wasn't her only goal. Joyner-Kersee also wanted to break her own world record.

The silver and bronze medalists each surpassed the Olympic record in the heptathlon. But neither came close to beating Joyner-Kersee. She won gold by a staggering 394 points. And she shattered the world record by 76 points. Five days after the heptathlon, she added a gold in the women's long jump. Then, at the 1992 Games in Barcelona, Spain, Joyner-Kersee successfully defended her gold medal in the heptathlon. She also won bronze in the long jump at those Games and at the 1996 Olympics in Atlanta.

Joyner-Kersee wasn't the only American woman to put on a historic display at the 1988 Games. Sprinter Florence Griffith Joyner, also known as "FloJo," had already set a world record in the US Olympic Trials. At the Games, she ran the 100-meter final just shy of her world-record time. But it was still enough for her to win gold.

Griffith Joyner put on an even better performance in the 200-meter final. She held a slight lead at the turn before the homestretch. She then stormed down the straightaway to win gold. Griffith Joyner also shattered the world record by 0.22 seconds. Both records still stood after the 2024 Olympics.

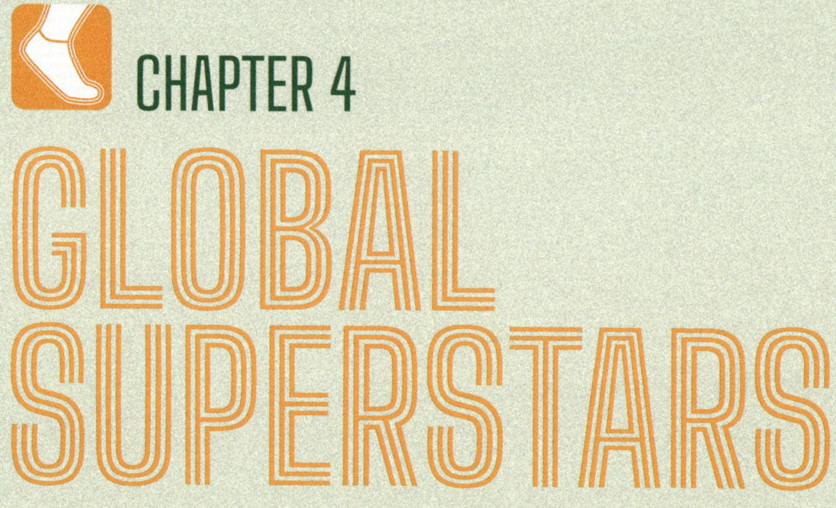

CHAPTER 4
GLOBAL SUPERSTARS

A new generation of US track-and-field stars emerged at the 1984 Olympics in Los Angeles. None of those athletes shined brighter than Carl Lewis. The son of two track-and-field coaches, Lewis seemed destined for greatness in the sport. He qualified for the 1980 Olympics at 19 years old. However, the United States boycotted those Games in Moscow, Soviet Union, due to the host's invasion of Afghanistan in 1979.

Lewis made sure his Olympic debut was worth the wait. At the 1984 Games, Lewis competed in four events. He won gold in the men's 100, 200, and long jump. Then he anchored the US team to a world record in the 4x100-meter race. Lewis's four golds replicated the performance of his idol Jesse Owens.

Unlike Owens, Lewis got the chance to compete in multiple Olympics. In 1988, he became the first man to defend his title in the 100. He added another gold in the long jump as well.

After winning gold in the men's 100-meter final at the 1984 Olympics, Carl Lewis celebrated by running around the track waving an American flag.

Then at the 1992 Games in Barcelona, Lewis helped break the 4x100 world record again. In the long jump, he faced off with the world record holder, American Mike Powell. Lewis edged out his teammate to win gold by three centimeters (1.2 in). Lewis finished his Olympic career with a fourth straight long jump gold at the 1996 Games in Atlanta. That gave him nine golds and 10 total medals. In 1999, *Sports Illustrated* magazine named Lewis its "Olympian of the Century."

By 1992, many people expected Michael Johnson to take over as the United States' next great sprinter. However, he got food poisoning two weeks before the Games. After losing a lot of weight, Johnson ended up not qualifying for any individual finals. But he did help the United States win gold in the 4x400-meter relay.

Johnson bounced back for the 1996 Games. And he made his intentions clear by wearing all gold track spikes. In the men's 400-meter final, Johnson set a new Olympic record on his way to gold. Then he smashed his own 200-meter world record by 0.34 seconds to claim another gold. Johnson went on to become the first Olympian to defend his 400 title at the 2000 Games in Sydney, Australia.

A new American star emerged at the 2004 Olympics in Athens. Allyson Felix won silver in the women's 200-meter at 18 years old. Four years later in Beijing, Felix won silver

Team USA's Michael Johnson was nicknamed "The Duck" because of his distinct running style.

in the same event. In each race, she lost to Jamaica's Veronica Campbell Brown. The two sprinters battled again at the 2012 Games in London. This time, though, Felix beat Campbell Brown to win her first individual Olympic gold medal.

Felix also helped the United States win gold in the women's 4x100 and 4x400 relays in 2012. She then won gold in both relays again at the 2016 Games in Rio. Felix qualified for her fifth Olympics when she was 35. At the Tokyo Games in 2021, she won her fourth straight gold in the 4x400. Felix ended her career with 11 medals, which made her the most decorated female Olympic track-and-field athlete.

JAMAICAN SPEED

Jamaica has a rich history in Olympic track and field. Arthur Wint won the country's first gold medal in the sport in 1948. After that, Jamaican athletes often took home medals each Olympics. Going into the 2008 Games, though, Jamaica had never won gold in the 100-meter. Usain Bolt changed that in Beijing. Then Shelly-Ann Fraser-Pryce won the country's first gold in the women's 100 two days later. Her teammates Sherone Simpson and Kerron Stewart tied to each win silver. Suddenly, Jamaica had become a sprinting powerhouse.

At the 2012 Olympics, Jamaica proved that 2008 hadn't been a fluke. Bolt led a Jamaican podium sweep in the men's 200-meter. Fraser-Pryce also defended her 100 title in a tight finish. At about 5 feet tall, Fraser-Pryce ran a completely different style than the much taller Bolt. She pumped her legs quickly to zoom down the track.

Fraser-Pryce and Bolt inspired a new generation of Jamaican sprinters. One of them was Elaine Thompson-Herah. Despite being cut from her high school track team, Thompson-Herah made her Olympic debut at the 2016 Games. There she beat Fraser-Pryce to become the new 100-meter champion. Thompson-Herah then took the 200 crown as well. That made her the first woman since Florence Griffith Joyner to win the 100 and 200 at the same Games.

Thompson-Herah headed into the Tokyo Games in 2021 with the chance to pull off a double again. She started that pursuit with a bang. In the 100 final, she ran neck and neck with Fraser-Pryce. But a late surge led to Thompson-Herah

From left, Jamaica's Veronica Campbell Brown, Shelly-Ann Fraser-Pryce, Christania Williams, and Elaine Thompson-Herah pose with their silver medals at the 2016 Olympics.

setting a new Olympic record of 10.61 seconds. Fraser-Pryce and Sherika Jackson rounded out a Jamaican podium sweep in the event. Thompson-Herah went on to defend her gold in the 200 three days later. That made her the first woman to win a double at two different Olympics.

MODERN STARS

The 2016 Olympics featured multiple athletes who turned into stars. Many track-and-field fans already knew Eliud Kipchoge before those Games. The Kenyan had won medals in the men's 5,000-meter at the 2004 and 2008 Games. Heading into 2016, Kipchoge had become one of the best marathoners in the world. Whenever he ran in a major marathon, he usually won.

The men's marathon in Rio was no different. Kipchoge won the race by more than a minute. He then defended his gold in dominant fashion at the Tokyo Games in 2021. Kipchoge became only the third man to win two straight Olympic marathon titles.

CZECH DOMINANCE

Jan Železný of the former Czechoslovakia began a dominant run in the men's javelin starting in 1988. After winning silver that year in Seoul, he went on to win gold in the event at the next three Olympics. At the 2008 Games, Barbora Špotáková became the first Czech woman to win gold in the javelin since 1952. She went on to defend her title at the 2012 Olympics in London.

Eliud Kipchoge of Kenya won the men's marathon at the Tokyo Olympics in 2021 with a time of 2:08:38.

Nafissatou Thiam had been dreaming of becoming an Olympic champion in the heptathlon long before 2016. The Belgian athlete began practicing for all the heptathlon events when she was just seven years old. Once the 2016 Games in Rio came around, 21-year-old Thiam was facing defending Olympic and world champion Jessica Ennis-Hill of Great Britain. But that didn't seem to scare Thiam. With strong results in the high jump, long jump, and shot put, Thiam upset Ennis-Hill to win gold. Thiam became the youngest heptathlon Olympic champion. She then defended her title in 2021 and 2024 to become the first athlete to ever win three straight gold medals in the heptathlon.

At the 2024 Olympics, American Ryan Crouser beat silver medalist Joe Kovacs in the men's shot put final by 0.75 meters (2.5 ft).

American Ryan Crouser seemed destined to be an Olympian. His dad was an alternate for Team USA in 1984. He also had an uncle and a cousin who were Olympians. None of them had the success that Crouser had, though. The American burst onto the Olympic scene in 2016 when he won gold in the men's shot put. Then at the Tokyo Games in 2021, his best throw went 23.30 meters (76.4 ft), setting a new Olympic record and earning him another gold.

CROWD FAVORITE

Sweden's Armand "Mondo" Duplantis set the world record in men's pole vault more than a year before the Tokyo Olympics in 2021. With no fans in the stands at those Games, though, Duplantis didn't break his own record. But he did win gold. Three years later at the Paris Games, Duplantis defended his Olympic title on his fourth jump. Before his sixth and final jump, the crowd of 69,000 fans clapped in unison. Then they roared as Duplantis cleared the bar at 6.25 meters (20.5 ft) to break his own world record.

In the years after the Tokyo Games, Crouser suffered multiple injuries. Three months before the 2024 Games in Paris, he tore a muscle in his chest. Yet, he still competed in the Olympics and blew away his competition. Crouser's gold in Paris made him the first man to win three straight Olympic shot put titles. Fellow American Joe Kovacs may have had some Olympic golds himself if it weren't for Crouser. In all three Games Crouser won gold, Kovacs earned the silver medal.

Sydney McLaughlin-Levrone did not win any medals at the 2016 Olympics. Just making it to those Games was a massive achievement, though. At only 16 years old, McLaughlin-Levrone was the youngest American track-and-field athlete to qualify for the Games in 36 years. When she returned for the Tokyo Olympics in 2021, she became a household name.

McLaughlin-Levrone's teammate Dalilah Muhammad had won gold in the women's 400-meter hurdles in 2016. At the US Olympic Trials in 2021, McLaughlin-Levrone broke Muhammad's world record. Then in Tokyo, McLaughlin-Levrone broke that record again to edge Muhammad for gold.

By the 2024 Games, some track-and-field analysts thought Femke Bol of the Netherlands could take the 400-meter hurdles title from McLaughlin-Levrone. The two were neck and neck in the first half of the Olympic final. Then McLaughlin-Levrone left Bol in the dust in the final half of the race. She broke her own world record and defended her title with a time of 50.37 seconds. And she won by 1.5 seconds. After the dominant performance, McLaughlin-Levrone took a victory lap with a tiara on her head. Her sister-in-law had given it to her to show people McLaughlin-Levrone's status as the queen of the 400-meter hurdles.

Along with her gold in the 400-meter hurdles, Sydney McLaughlin-Levrone helped Team USA win gold in the women's 4x400 relay at the 2024 Olympics.

GLOSSARY

alternate
A replacement athlete who is eligible to compete in an event in case another athlete is unable to do so.

amateur
A person who plays a sport without getting paid.

anchor
The last competitor for a team in a relay.

boycott
To refuse to take part in an event as a form of protest.

debut
First appearance.

dictator
A person with complete control of a country.

doping
Using illegal substances to boost one's performance.

double
In track, when an athlete wins gold in two different individual events.

elite
The highest level.

fluke
An unlikely event that occurs thanks to a stroke of luck.

heat
An early race in a championship meet that determines which athletes qualify for the finals.

iconic
Well-known for excellence.

polio
An infectious disease that attacks the brain and spinal cord, often of young children.

steeplechase
A race in which runners must jump over hurdles and into water once a lap.

sweep
When one country wins all three medals in an event.

MORE INFORMATION

BOOKS

McDougall, Chrös. *The Olympics Encyclopedia*. Abdo, 2022.

Price, Karen. *GOATs of Olympic Sports*. Abdo, 2022.

Stevenson, Robin. *Kid Olympians, Summer*. Quirk, 2024.

ONLINE RESOURCES

To learn more about Olympic track and field, please visit **abdobooklinks.com** or scan this QR code. These links are routinely monitored and updated to provide the most current information available.

INDEX

ABOUT THE AUTHOR

Luke Hanlon is a sportswriter and editor who lives in Minneapolis, Minnesota. He's covered multiple Olympic sports for TeamUSA.org.